Copyright © 2018 by Ingo Blum
Published by planet!oh concepts gmbh
PO Box 19 01 40, 50498 Cologne, Germany

ISBN: 978-1-982958-22-0

Cover and chapter Illustrations by Antonio Pahetti
Copy design and book layout by Emy Farella

Go to **www.ingoblum.com** and get
a book for **FREE**!

INGO BLUM

BIG

It Takes So Little To Be Big

The famous Circus Wilson was a guest in a small village.

There were wild animals and clowns, artists and musicians, jugglers and acrobats, and fire-eaters and knife-throwers in that circus.

The tiniest animal, however, was little Lee the flea.

Lee was an artist.

He could perform a four-time somersault and jump through the burning eye of a needle.

The problem was his size. Only his glittering pants showed the audience where he was.

"There he is!" cried the children.

"I cannot see him!" shouted others.

"Just try, he is a flea!"

"Ugh . . . I don't like fleas! They bite."

"Look at that glittering!"

Very often the other animals laughed about him, too.

"You are not dangerous enough," the tigers told him.

"You cannot run as fast as we can," the horses neighed.

"You are not funny enough," the clowns giggled.

"But I do not want to be dangerous and fast and funny," Lee replied.

He just wanted to be **BIGGER**.

One day, he made a decision to change his life.

A few days later, the circus crossed a big forest and arrived in another village.

Again, it was a successful performance. At the end, when it was time for Lee the flea to perform, no one could find him. There was no trace of Lee.

Lee the flea was gone.

Everybody looked for him.

Everybody was concerned.

But nobody found him.

"Perhaps he ended up in a visitor's hair,"
said one of the artists.

"Hopefully, nobody sat on him," worried a
knife-thrower.

"By accident, of course!"
the clowns giggled.

Soon, Director Wilson left to go back into the big forest they had crossed before.

He saw a ranger who scraped wildly all over his body.

"Did you see my flea, Lee?" he asked the ranger.

The ranger laughed. "A flea? No, I have not seen him."

"Maybe he has bitten you and that is why you scrape so wildly."

"A mosquito has bitten me!"

Then he met a bear, who also scratched at his fur.

"Have you seen my flea, Lee?" he asked again.

The bear shook his head. Suddenly, a bee emerged from the bear's fur and flew away.

The bear had taken her honey, so she had tried to sting him.

Some children were playing hide and seek in the forest.

"Have you seen my flea, Lee?" director Wilson asked once again.

"We have not seen him. Come play with us," the children cried.

"Why are you scratching?" the director asked a boy.

"It tickles me!"

"Maybe it's Lee. Be careful!"

But then a small spider crawled over the boy's arm and ran down its long spider cord to the ground.

Director Wilson was sad.

He had searched far and wide but no Lee.

He lay down on a large stone to rest for a moment.

"Mr. Director, Mr. Director!" Somebody called for him.

Director Wilson opened his eyes and blinked. Lee the flea sat on the leaf of a bush and watched him.

"There you are, Lee. I've been looking for you everywhere," said Wilson.

"I broke out to ask myself some questions," Lee said.

"What questions?" the director asked.

"Questions about my life."

"I always wanted to be a big artist, but people laugh at me and only see my glittering pants, not my tricks. I am not dangerous like the tigers, not funny enough like the clowns, and I cannot run like the horses."

"You do not have to!" Director Wilson said.

"No, but I want to be seen! Look, I have an idea.
Let me tell you."

Director Wilson listened.

Everyone was glad when the lost ones returned.

The next day the show went on.

A huge magnifying glass was placed in front of the audience.

"What is that?" somebody asked.

"Look through the magnifier!" Director Wilson said.

"It's a flea!"

"He is so . . . BIG!"

Like a wild firefly, Lee made a few somersaults, juggled, and ran across a thread, which was stretched across the circus ring. Finally, he hopped through a burning needle's eye.

Outstanding!

"That is a new sensation," Director Wilson said.

It was true. Everybody could see Lee's tricks now. Soon, he became a big star.

Whatever **BIG** was . . .

Lee The Flea Coloring Pics

More Reading and Coloring Fun

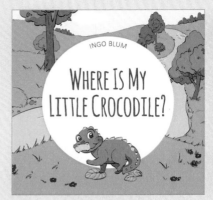

ISBN 978-1-982941-28-4

ISBN 978-1-982941-74-1

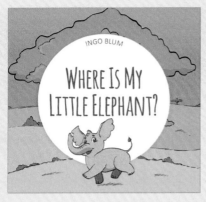

ISBN 978-1-982941-88-8

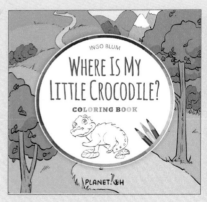

ISBN 978-3-947410-21-7

ISBN 978-3-947410-23-1

ISBN 978-1-723891-09-0

ISBN 978-1-983075-91-9

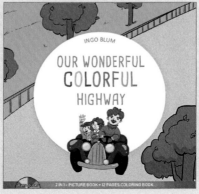

ISBN 978-3-947410-56-9

ISBN 978-1-982942-12-0

Thank You

Thank you for reading this little story. I hope you enjoyed it the same way I did while writing it. If you would like to know when my next book comes out, find more books I have written, and receive some occasional updates from me, just visit me on my website.

www.ingoblum.com

Do you find reader reviews helpful? If so, please spare a moment to help me by rating this book, so others will find it (and read it!), too.

I always appreciate an honest review.

Looking forward to your letters, comments, and opinions.
All the best, Ingo

About the Author

Ingo Blum is a German author and comedian. His journey to become a children's book author began during his day job. He has always enjoyed projects where he could create artwork for kids. He started writing stories to accompany these projects for fun, and with some encouragement from friends and family (and their kids!), he decided to share his stories with the world. Ingo works with international illustrators with whom he constantly develops new concepts and stories.

About the Illustrator

Antonio Pahetti is a young artist with a lot of experience in children's illustration, who makes his illustrations with much love and a passion for details. His works are published in many countries. He lives in the Ukraine.

Made in the USA
San Bernardino, CA
22 July 2019